by Lily Browne
illustrated by Maggie Dannatt

SCHOOL PUBLISHERS

Printed in China

ISBN 10: 0-15-351364-0
ISBN 13: 978-0-15-351364-0

Ordering Options
ISBN 10: 0-15-351211-3 (Grade 1 Advanced Collection)
ISBN 13: 978-0-15-351211-7 (Grade 1 Advanced Collection)
ISBN 10: 0-15-358042-9 (package of 5)
ISBN 13: 978-0-15-358042-0 (package of 5)

4 5 6 7 8 9 10 0940 15 14 13 12 11 10 09

"I am going to take you for a picnic tomorrow," Mom said to the children. "We will go to the beach, and you can take Kate's kite to fly."

"My kite is ripped," said Kate. "I'll have to make a new one."

"I'll help," said Luke. "I am good at building kites. We made a kite at school, so I know what to do."

"I'll help, too," said Grace. "I like making things."

3

Luke found a piece of plastic. He
cut out a fish shape.

Kate found two sticks. She crossed
them over and held them together
with string. "This is the frame for the
fish kite," she said.

Grace found some tape. She taped
the plastic fish to the frame.

Then Kate found some cloth for
the fish kite's tail. Luke helped Kate
tie pieces of cloth to the string. The
kite's tail grew longer and longer.

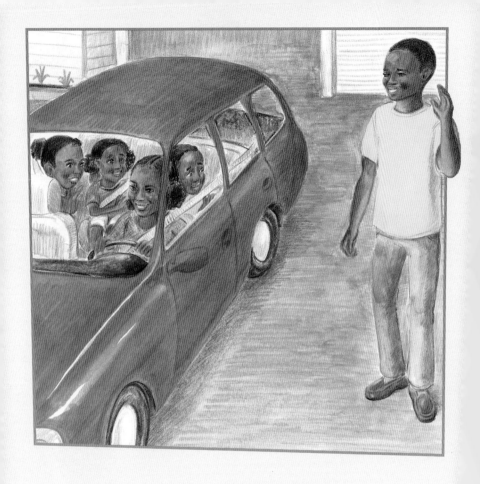

The next day, Mom and the
children waved to Dad as they left.

"Have fun!" called Dad.

"Toot, toot," went the car horn.

Then they drove toward the beach
in the car.

At the beach, a boy from school
was flying his kite. He gave Luke, Kate,
and Grace a welcoming wave.

"Fly your kite beside mine," called
the boy.

The children's fish kite went up
and up. It fluttered and flapped and
swooped in the wind like a darting
fish. Then it flew down into the sea.

"Your kite is all wet," Mom said to the children who had waded into the shallow water to get it back.

"Our kite is a flying fish," joked the children. "It likes to fly *and* swim!"

8